For Lucas.

With special thanks to Chris and Rod.

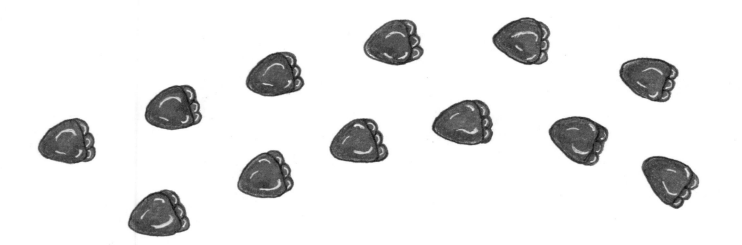

Crack,

Crack,

Crack.

A nest is full of eggs and one of them is hatching.
It cracked and cracked and cracked, what could it be that's scratching?

Roar,

Roar,

Roar!

A Little Dinosaur appeared and jumped out of the nest.
It roared and roared and roared, because that's what it does best.

Bounce, Bounce, Bounce.

The Little Dinosaur bounced around, in grass so bright and green.
He bounced and bounced and bounced, the highest he'd ever been.

Stomp,

Stomp,

Stomp.

The Little Dinosaur began to stomp, over a giant hill.
He stomped and stomped and stomped so far, he began
to feel quite ill.

Splish,

Splash,

Splosh.

The Little Dinosaur splashed around, in a giant puddle of mud.

He splished and splashed and sploshed so much,

that he fell with a great big thud.

Sniff,

Sniff,

Sniff.

The Little Dinosaur wandered into a field of wild flowers.

He sniffed and sniffed and sniffed, he played in there for hours.

Aaaa, Aaaa, Aaaachooo.

The Little Dinosaur sniffed a dandelion clock and he began to sneeze.

He sneezed and sneezed and sneezed,

making the seeds fly into the breeze.

Scrunch, Scrunch,

Scrunch.

The Little Dinosaur began to walk along the leaf covered ground.

It scrunched and scrunched and scrunched,

he did not like the horrid sound.

Yawn,

Yawn,

Yawn.

The Little Dinosaur started to feel alone and very sleepy.

He yawned and yawned and yawned, he began to feel quite weepy.

Twit, Twit, Twoo.

"Who are you?" asked an Owl way up in the tree.

"I am Little Dinosaur and I'm lost, can you help me?"

Flap, Flap, Flap.

The Owl began to flap its wings, as it guided the Dinosaur home.

It flapped and flapped and flapped,

now the Dinosaur wasn't alone.

The Little Dinosaur followed the Owl,

back over the leaf covered ground.

Then past the dandelion clock seeds,

that the Little Dinosaur had found.

The Owl then showed Little Dinosaur

the way through the field of flowers.

Then past the giant puddle of mud, this could take them hours.

The Owl led the Little Dinosaur over the giant hill.
Then past the grass so bright and green, the adventure was such a thrill.

The Owl then found the Little Dinosaur's warm and cosy nest.

Little Dinosaur smiled at Owl,

then climbed on in, for a well-deserved rest.

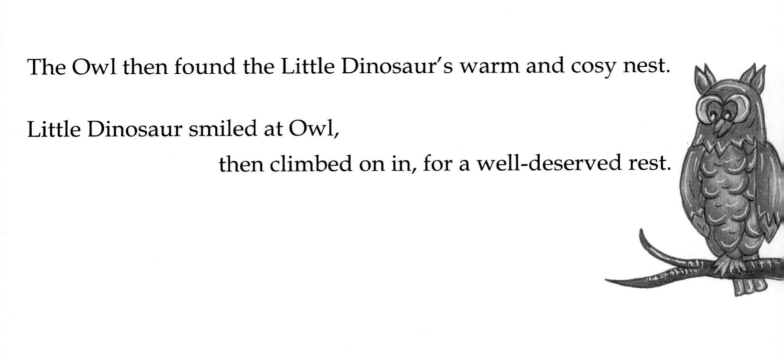

ISBN 978-1-9996059-0-2

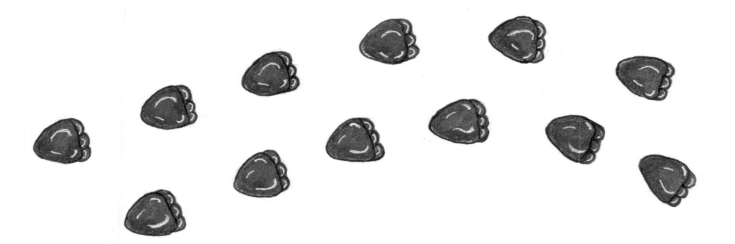

Made in the USA
San Bernardino, CA
11 April 2019